When I grow up,
I'm going to play for ...

the **MICHIGAN STATE SPARTANS!™**

First published by Hometown World in the United Kingdom, 2016

Published in the United States by Sourcebooks, Inc.
Sourcebooks and the colophon are registered trademarks of Sourcebooks, Inc.

Published by Sourcebooks Jabberwocky, an imprint of Sourcebooks, Inc.
P.O. Box 4410, Naperville, Illinois 60567-4410
(630) 961-3900
Fax: (630) 961-2168
jabberwockykids.com

Date of Production: June 2016
Run Number: HTW_PO040416
Printed and bound in China (GD)
10 9 8 7 6 5 4 3 2 1

When I grow up, I'm going to play for... the MICHIGAN STATE SPARTANS!™

Written by Gemma Cary
Illustrated by Tatio Viana and Adrian Bijloo

sourcebooks
jabberwocky

"Out you go,"

said Mom, and the screen went black.

"No!" shouted Jack.

SCORE: 4   TIME: 2:00

10

"I was winning!"
"Very good," said Mom. "Now go
and play outside."
Jack glanced at the window and saw
his cat, Furball, scowling in the rain.
"But ..."

Soon Jack found himself outside, standing in a puddle.
What was he supposed to do out here? His football was
flat and there was no one to play with.

"I know!" he said, stomping inside.
If there was no one to play football with, he could still practice with a different ball.

Jack went into his bedroom to get a ball.
On the back of his door, he saw his
favorite shirt: his Michigan State
Spartans jersey.

He always felt more confident wearing his favorite jersey, and so he usually played better, too.

Back outside, it had stopped raining. Jack got ready to take the snap.

He stepped back in the pocket and looked for an open receiver.

He dodged the pass rush, then got ready to throw the ball deep downfield.

The ball sailed over the fence and hit something with a satisfying

thwack.

"Owww!"

squealed old Mrs. Crabapple,
who had been busy digging up carrots.
"My bottom!"

Just then, Jack heard the familiar thump of a car door.

"Hello, Mrs. Crabapple," called Jack's dad, appearing in the backyard. Mrs. Crabapple scowled and speared the tennis ball with her hefty pitchfork. "Sorry," said Jack, trying not to laugh.

"Hello, Superstar!"

Dad held out a bag and Jack peered inside. It was a brand-new football!

"Wow, thanks!" said Jack. "I noticed your old football was flat," said Dad, "so I got you a new one to keep practicing with."

Whoooooosh!

The pair were soon playing their best-ever game of football. Time seemed to fly as fast as their passes!

When they stopped for lunch, Dad said, "All your practice is really paying off, Jack. I've talked to our local team. They're having a tryout tomorrow, and they said you can come along, if you want to."

"Really?"
said Jack.
"Awesome!"

The next day, father and son arrived at the football field. The locker room was filled with children in blue and red uniforms, nervously waiting to show off their skills.

The coach soon signaled for Jack to join a game, and Jack raced over. He cheered when players scored a touchdown and encouraged others who dropped the ball. When one boy slipped and fell, Jack helped him up.

But secretly, Jack was worried about his own performance. When the halftime whistle blew, he had barely touched the ball, let alone scored.

Someone near the bench caught Jack's eye.
It was his **dad**, waving at him. Jack jogged
over and his **dad** pulled his Michigan State
Spartans jersey from a backpack.

"I'm proud of you, son. You've been a real team player today! I thought you might want to wear your favorite jersey. Go show them what you can do!"

Jack did as his dad said. As he sprinted back onto the field, he imagined he was stepping out of the tunnel at Spartan Stadium. Green-and-white banners rippled through the air while the crowd sang the team's fight song.

In the second half, Jack was one of the best players
on the field! He scored three touchdowns, including
an incredible leaping catch over two defenders.
He was confident. He was happy. He was ...

PLAYING LIKE A STAR!

At the end of the tryout, the coach called out
the names of players who had made the final cut:
"Danny, Oliver, Leo ..."
Everyone clapped after each name.
"Joe, Sam, Joshua ..."

Jack stared at his feet. Maybe he hadn't made the team after all. "Freddie, Zac, Harry, Ben ..."

"Waaahoooo!"

Jack leaped into the air, waving his arms in excitement.

"I'll take that as a 'yes'," said the coach, and everyone laughed.

Dad couldn't stop grinning. He praised Jack all the way home. "You were amazing, son! Unstoppable. A real champion!"

"Thanks, Dad," Jack replied. "I can't wait for my first game. But one day I suppose I won't be able to play for them anymore."

"Oh? Why not?" asked Dad.

"Because when I grow up, I'm going to play for the Michigan State Spartans!"

Can you guess who else is going to play for the Michigan State Spartans?

You
are!

MICHIGAN STATE SPARTANS' NEXT SUPERSTAR!

Stick your photo here

Write your name here

....

....

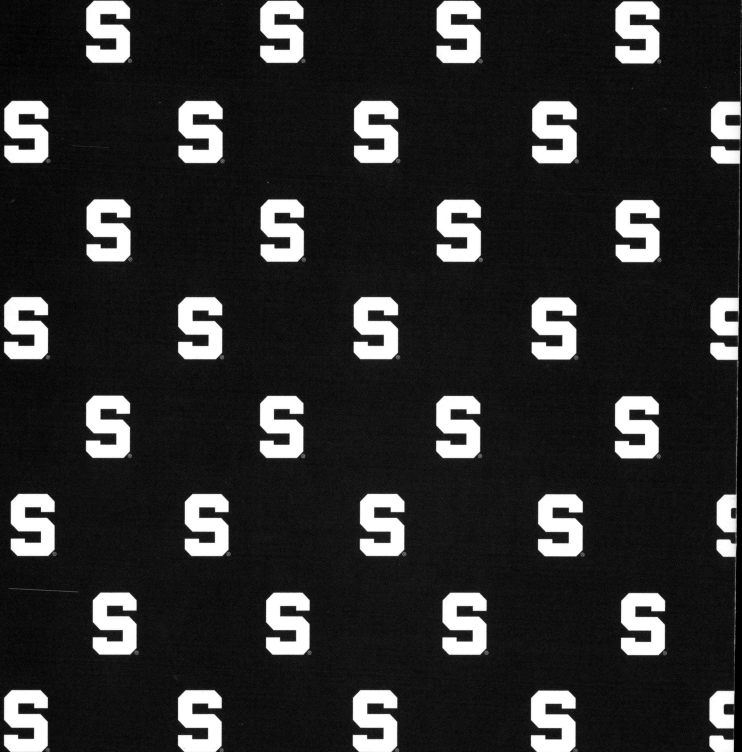